Poppleton

IN FALL

Read more
Poppleton
books!

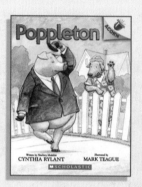

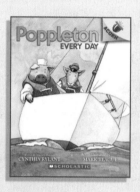

Poppleton
IN FALL

Written by Newbery Medalist

Illustrated by

CYNTHIA RYLANT   MARK TEAGUE

ACORN™
SCHOLASTIC INC.

Library of Congress Cataloging-in-Publication Data

Names: Rylant, Cynthia, author. | Teague, Mark, illustrator. | Rylant, Cynthia. Poppleton ; 4.
Title: Poppleton in fall / written by Newbery Medalist Cynthia Rylant ; illustrated by Mark Teague.
Description: [New edition]. | New York : Acorn/Scholastic Inc., 2020. | Series: Poppleton ; 4 | Originally published in 1999 by The Blue Sky Press. | Summary: Poppleton the pig enjoys the company of geese flying south, buys a new winter coat with the help of his friend Cherry Sue, and tries to order pancakes at the Lion's Club breakfast.
Identifiers: LCCN 2018055640| ISBN 9781338566734 (pb) | ISBN 9781338566741 (hc) | ISBN 9781338566826 (ebk)
Subjects: LCSH: Poppleton (Fictitious character) — Juvenile fiction. | Swine — Juvenile fiction. | Animals — Juvenile fiction. | Friendship — Juvenile fiction. | Autumn — Juvenile fiction. | CYAC: Pigs — Fiction. | Animals — Fiction. | Friendship — Fiction. | Autumn — Fiction.
Classification: LCC PZ7.R982 Pwe 2020 | DDC 813.54 [E] — dc23
LC record available at https://lccn.loc.gov/2018055640

10 9 8 7 6 5 4 3 2 1   20 21 22 23 24

Printed in China   62
This edition first printing, July 2020
Book design by Maria Mercado

CONTENTS

MEET THE CHARACTERS

Poppleton

Cherry Sue

Zacko

THE GEESE

One fall day
Poppleton saw two geese
flying south over his house.

"Hello, geese!" called Poppleton.
"Would you like some cookies?"

"Thanks!" said the geese,
and they landed.

Their names were Ted and Ned.

Poppleton enjoyed them very much
and was sad to see them go.

But soon after,
Poppleton saw five geese
flying south over his house.

"Hello, geese!" called Poppleton.
"Would you like some cookies?"

"You bet!" said the geese,
and they landed.

Their names were Mary, Sherry,
Harry, Larry, and Jerry.

They all knew Ted and Ned.

Poppleton enjoyed them very much
and was sad to see them go.

But soon after,
Poppleton saw eight geese
flying south over his house.

"Hello, geese!" Poppleton called.
"Would you like some cookies?"
(He hoped he had enough.)

"Would we ever!" said the geese,
and they landed.

Their names were Ann, Stan, Dan,
Fran, Han, Jan, Nan, and Van.

Poppleton enjoyed them very much
and was sad to see them go.

Because he was feeling a little lonely,
he went to visit his neighbor Cherry Sue.

"Hello, Poppleton!" said Cherry Sue.
"What's new?"

"Too zoo moo poo boo coo do,"
said Poppleton.

"You'd better go take a nap,"
said Cherry Sue.

And he did.

THE COAT

The days were getting chilly.
Poppleton needed a new coat.

17

He went to see his friend Zacko
at the coat store.

"I need a new coat, Zacko,"
Poppleton said.

"Good!" said Zacko.
"Let me measure you."

Zacko measured
Poppleton from
head
to
toe.

Zacko measured
Poppleton from
side to side.

Zacko measured
Poppleton
all around.

Zacko shook his head.

"I have nothing to fit you, Poppleton,"
said Zacko.

"Nothing to fit me?" cried Poppleton.

"You are too big," said Zacko.

"I am not!" cried Poppleton.
And he stormed out the door.

At home, Poppleton looked at himself
in the mirror.

He
looked
head
to
toe.

He looked side to side.

He looked
all around.

He got depressed.

Cherry Sue was walking by.
She saw Poppleton through the window.

"What's wrong, Poppleton?"
Cherry Sue asked.

"I am too big," said Poppleton glumly.

"Says who?" said Cherry Sue.

"Says Zacko," said Poppleton.

"Zacko's a ferret!" said Cherry Sue.

"I know that," said Poppleton.

"So of course he thinks you're too big!"
cried Cherry Sue.
"Did you tell him he's too small?"

"No," said Poppleton.

"Because you have good manners,"
said Cherry Sue.

"You are a big pig, Poppleton!" she said.
"Be proud!"

"I would like to be proud in a **coat**,"
said Poppleton.
"And Zacko has only small ones."

"Posh," said Cherry Sue.
"Wait here."

She hurried home.

Soon she was back with a catalog.

Poppleton read the title:
BIG AND TALL PIGS.

"I get all the catalogs," said Cherry Sue.
"Even the ones for mice."

"Gee, thanks!" said Poppleton.

When the new coat arrived,
Poppleton slowly walked past
Zacko's store.

He looked very big.
He looked very proud.

But then he felt sorry for Zacko,
being so small.

So Poppleton went in and bought a scarf.

PANCAKE BREAKFAST

Each fall the Lions Club
had a pancake breakfast.

Poppleton loved this.
If anyone could make a pancake,
it was a lion.

So Poppleton invited Cherry Sue,
and they dressed their best
and went to breakfast.

When they arrived,
the lions were flipping pancakes like crazy
and calling out,
"Buckwheat! Cinnamon! Johnnycake!
Spicy nut! Apple! Banana! Blueberry!"

"What flavor do you want, Cherry Sue?"
asked Poppleton.

"Plain," said Cherry Sue.

"Plain?" asked Poppleton.
"You can make plain at home!"

"I like plain," said Cherry Sue.

"You probably like vanilla ice cream, too,"
said Poppleton.

"Love it," said Cherry Sue.

"All right. Wait here.
I'll get you a plain pancake,"
said Poppleton.

He went up to a lion.

"Are you making plain pancakes?"
Poppleton asked.

"ARE YOU KIDDING?" the lion roared.

"Sorry!" cried Poppleton, moving on.

He went up to another lion.

"Do you have any plain pancakes?"
Poppleton asked.

"ARE YOU JOKING?" the lion roared.

"Sorry!" cried Poppleton, moving on.

He went up to a third lion.

"Plain pancake, please,"
Poppleton said in a small voice.

"NO!" the lion roared.

Poppleton went back to Cherry Sue.

"Where's my pancake?" she asked.

"Try blueberry," said Poppleton.

"Why?" asked Cherry Sue.

"Just try blueberry," said Poppleton.

"Why?" asked Cherry Sue.

"JUST TRY BLUEBERRY!"
yelled Poppleton.

"WHY?" yelled Cherry Sue.

"BECAUSE THEY'RE GOING TO EAT ME
IF I ORDER PLAIN!" yelled Poppleton.

Cherry Sue thought.

"Blueberry will be perfect," she said.

And it was.

"You are a **perfect** friend,"
Poppleton said on the way home.

"I know," said Cherry Sue.

ABOUT THE CREATORS

CYNTHIA RYLANT

has written more than one hundred books, including *Dog Heaven, Cat Heaven,* and the Newbery Medal–winning novel *Missing May.* She lives with her pets in Oregon.

MARK TEAGUE

lives in New York State with his family, which includes a dog and two cats, but no pigs, llamas, or goats, and only an occasional mouse. Mark is the author of many books and the illustrator of many more, including the How Do Dinosaurs series.

YOU CAN DRAW

1. Draw a pickle shape. (Sketch lightly so you can erase as you go!)

2. Add arms and feet.

3. Ovals make Zacko's head and hands.

4. Add ears and draw Zacko's face. Give him a smile!

ZACKO!

5. Fill out his arms and hands. Begin to sketch his suit.

6. Add details to his suit.

7. Add buttons, a tail, and fur. That's Zacko!

8. Color in your drawing!

WHAT'S YOUR STORY?

Poppleton's geese friends fly south for the winter.
Imagine **you** could go somewhere for the winter.
Where would you go?
What would you bring with you?
Write and draw your story!